HILLTOP ELEMENTARY SCHOOL

Country Kid,
City Kid

Country Kid, City Kid

JULIE CUMMINS ♦ Illustrations by TED RAND

Henry Holt and Company
New York

Henry Holt and Company, LLC, *Publishers since 1866*
175 Fifth Avenue, New York, New York 10010
www.HenryHoltKids.com

Library of Congress Cataloging-in-Publication Data
Cummins, Julie.
Country kid, city kid / Julie Cummins; illustrations by Ted Rand.
Summary: Although Ben lives on a farm in the country and Jody lives in an
apartment in the city, when they meet at camp they find they have a lot in common.
[1. Country life—Fiction. 2. Farm life—Fiction.
3. City and town life—Fiction.] I. Rand, Ted, ill. II. Title.
PZ7.C9155 Co 2002   [E]—dc21   2001003846

ISBN 978-0-8050-6467-4
First Edition—2002
Printed in China by South China Printing Company Ltd.,
Dongguan City, Guangdong Province
9 10 8

Ben is a country kid. When he wakes up in the morning, he hears cows mooing and birds singing.

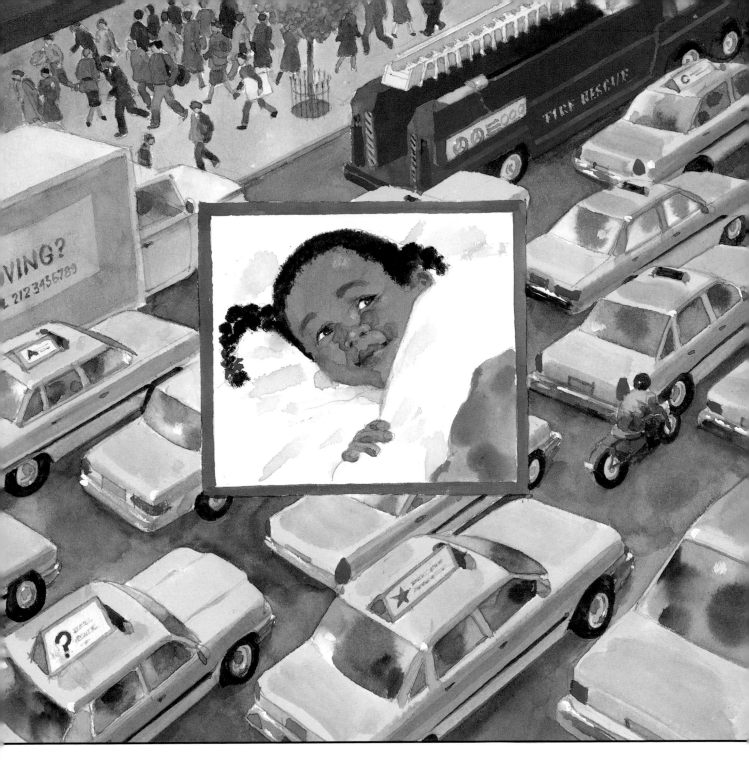

Jody is a city kid. When she wakes up in the morning, she hears taxicab horns and fire truck sirens.

Ben lives on a farm, where he and his family
raise cattle. From his bedroom window on the
second floor, he can see rows and rows of potatoes
and beans.

Jody lives in an apartment building with her mom and dad. From her bedroom window on the eighth floor, she can see tall skyscrapers and a busy city street filled with cars.

When Ben goes to school, he takes a school bus that drives many miles on country roads to pick up children.

When Jody leaves for school, her mom walks with
her to the bus stop where a crowded city bus takes
her to school.

At Ben's school, when it's time for recess the
kids race out to the big field behind the school
to play ball.

At Jody's school, the playground is surrounded
by a high fence that keeps kids from running into
the busy, crowded streets after escaping balls.

Ben goes grocery shopping with his mother once
a week. They drive to a large supermarket in the
nearest town and fill up two big shopping carts.

Jody and her mom walk to the little neighborhood
stores every few days to buy fresh vegetables, meat,
and bread. They carry the food home in plastic bags.

To see if his grandmother has sent him a birthday card, Ben has to walk out to the road where the mailbox stands.

Jody's mailbox is in a large wall unit in the lobby of the building. She needs a key to open it to look for her favorite magazine.

The first snowfall sends Ben scurrying for his sled to go sliding down the big hill with his friends.

When it snows in the city, Jody knows to
wear boots for walking on the slushy sidewalks.
She can't resist jumping in the fresh snow.

At Christmastime, Ben and his dad cut down
a pine tree from the woods behind the farm and
bring it home on the back of their truck.

Jody and her parents buy their Christmas tree
from a sidewalk vendor and take it home on top
of a taxicab.

When Ben needs to read about a famous person for a book report, his mom drives him to the book-mobile stop.

When Jody needs information for a school project, she and her dad visit the neighborhood library.

Every day when Ben gets home from school, his
pet collie eagerly greets him and races around while
he does his chores.

Jody's pet hamster is quiet, sleeps a lot, and exercises on a wheel in a small cage in her bedroom. She feeds him treats and lets him scamper on her bed while she's reading.

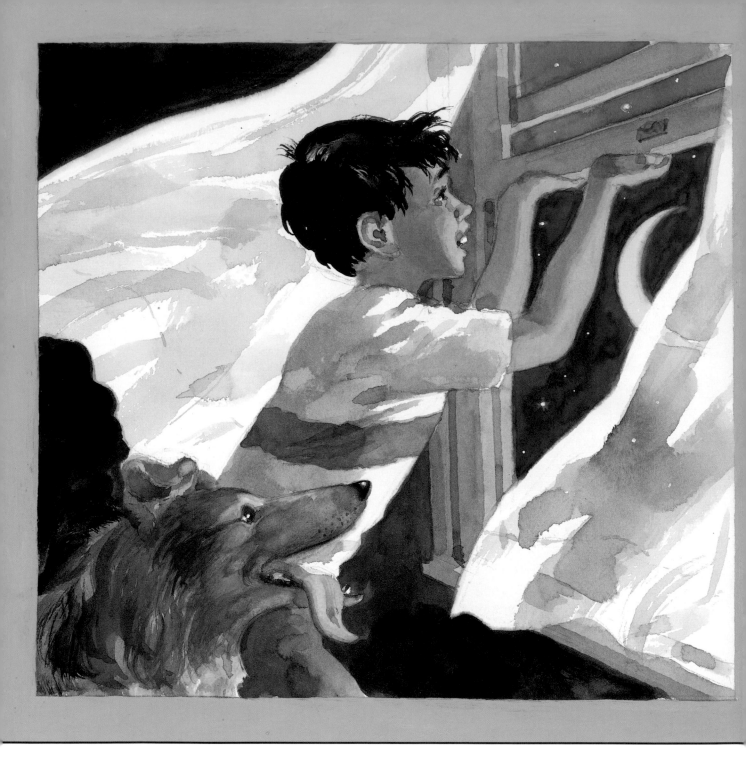

When it gets hot in the summer, Ben opens his bedroom window to let in cool breezes.

When it gets hot in the summer, Jody and her parents stay inside their air-conditioned apartment with the windows shut. Sometimes they go to an air-conditioned movie.

For summer vacation, Ben is eager to go to Camp Eagle Ridge to canoe, build campfires, and meet new friends.

Jody is excited about her first
time at Camp Eagle Ridge. She
looks forward to swimming, hiking,
and learning to ride a horse.

After meeting
their counselors and
checking out their cabins,
Jody and Ben join the
other campers in the
main hall. Ben and Jody
are paired as buddies for
a scavenger hunt, and they are very excited
when they find a four-leafed clover for their list.

Ben helps Jody climb on
and off a horse, and Jody helps
Ben braid his lanyard. Both of
them have lots of fun swimming
in the lake and learning how to paddle a canoe. They
win second place in the team canoeing competition.

On the last night of camp, the two new friends sing with the others around the campfire. They promise to keep in touch until they meet at camp again next year. They make plans to send each other e-mails, swap photos of their pets, and share favorite mystery stories.

As soon as Ben returns to his home in the country, he's going to draw a map of the constellations that he can see from his bedroom window to send to Jody. When Jody returns to the city, she is going to send Ben a street map of the city bus routes and mark where her favorite places are.

Country kid, city kid—
miles apart but two of a kind.